Tales the Crows Taught Me

Written by Laura Lovic-Lindsay

Dedication

It's all David's fault.

I said those same words all throughout our childhood (okay, sometimes it was Vernon's fault), but this time I really mean it.

My brother David goaded me for years, trying to get me to write. "I'm a *reader*. I don't write," I told him. But he's been a stubborn little shite since day one and kept at it.

Finally, when I was about thirty-five, raising two kids by myself I said, "Fine! I'll do it. I'll write a book. You'll see that it's rubbish and leave me alone."

So I started writing lists of what I loved to see in stories, novels. When my lists were done, I read them over and over. Gradually, the elements contained within gave rise to characters. Soon, I had twenty-plus chapters of a novel I loved.

I was writing. And it wasn't rubbish.

And I LOVED it.

All the worlds that had played in my brain for so long, found their way onto paper. And other people were digging it, too!

So, this collection gets dedicated to David, for decades of nagging and persevering.

Thanks for helping me discover my life's love, Smol One.

Table of Contents

SMALL ONYA

She tries to fool me, but I know what she is doing.

I see her muscles growing. She is strengthening herself. She will need stronger muscles in our right arm if she is to do it properly, do it quickly.

But my side has always been stronger. If Onya leaned properly, I could make us run. *She* could not do this. She resented this, and so she said it hurt to lean.

As children, I wanted to climb like the others. Onya was afraid. Her arm could not hold us, she said. She told Mother that I wanted to climb. Mother told me, "You are a fool. You will both be killed."

"I should think you would be pleased to have us killed," I mumbled.

It was *my* face she slapped. It was *my* arm she pinched until it blued and I cried.

Mother took Onya's side, in all ways. Mother took her hand when we walked, never mine, never walked my side. I was kept street-side. Mother yearned to see me trampled. She wished for it. She wanted the laughs and the pointing and the looks to fall upon me first. Keep Onya between us, protect her. Small Onya, who had no strength. Small Onya, who would not have lived on her own.

Me, I would have lived. I am bigger, stronger. I *feel* more of us. She might have been removed, taken off of me. Mother knew this, knew it when she sold us. Onya could have been removed and I would still have lived.

I could have climbed. I could have run.

We would not have been sold to the tall bloated man with the belly, mustache, and chain-watch, the man who made Mother take our double-dress from us. Made us stand while he regarded us, sniffing. Onya would not look at him, but I locked onto his ugly purple nose, his angry wrinkles, his mustache with fat and wax smeared through. I did glare at him until he broke gaze, looked away. He did not ask to see us that way again.

He made Mother bring us to him at the edge of the town. She cried and hugged us both, but kissed only Onya.

The angry man coughed and said, "When I speak to you, you will call me 'Sir' or 'Mr. Brighton.'"

We were not to speak to him unless he told us to do so. He told us this, and no more.

He put a blanket over us and made us ride in a carriage with no windows. In an hour, I heard voices, some shouting impatience, some excited. We heard swears and spitting. We heard the ringing hammers of the circus being taken apart and packed for the first time in our life. We smelled the tang of train-smoke.

Mr. Brighton gave us to the Lady Who Wore Flowers in Her Hair. She pulled our blanket from us and smiled the kindest smile. She said we must call *her* Mother now. And so we did. We were to live in her caravan. When she was not on her tightrope, she fed us, bathed us, told us stories, tickled us, taught us, loved us.

She held us both when we cried after the first time Mr. Brighton made us stand before the crowds. We were no strangers to whispers, to pointing. But these men gasped, some women moaned and streamed tears.

One man put his hand over his lady's eyes, praying loudly for God to destroy us. "Monster," he hissed. "Demon."

A man argued with Mr. Brighton that our clothes should be taken from us. He would not believe we were one unless he could see.

They argued for some time and then Mother was there in the corner. She called to us, and took my hand, pulled us behind red velveted curtains where she took flowers from her hair, put them in ours. Then she kissed us both on the nose. She said we did well and that we would not need to do that again until evening.

For years, Mr. Brighton stood us before crowds three times a day. Six, on weekends. Onya suffered this. But I grew angry, looking every man in the eyes. The women would not look at my face. Many times Mr. Brighton told Mother she must make me stop doing that. They argued.

My favorite times were between shows. We could lie on the hills surrounding us, if we were lucky enough to have hills that week, and tell the clouds to each other. We could play dolls under the tents, trickle soft sawdust through our hands. We could walk freely through tall grasses, among the tents and visit the others who, like us, stood on a stage while the people of the towns squinted their eyes, stared down their noses.

We were not allowed to go see towns. Mr.

4

Brighton chewed his cigar and spat, "Why, then, would they come and pay for what they can see for free?"

Onya did not want to go into those towns anyway. When we were fourteen, I tried to make her go with me. By now, we had our own caravan. Mother had married and had two young children of her own. She still smiled wide when she saw us. She had told us we must come see her whenever we liked. Her children held up their arms to us when we came near and called us "sister."

I held the youngest on my side, whispered in his ear that I would go to towns and bring back candy for them all.

Onya balked and made herself slow and heavy on my side. Still, I pulled her, made her walk. She did not like when I disobeyed Mr. Brighton. But I gave Onya no choice. I had a dollar in my pocket, left from our birthday. Onya had long spent hers. She craved the sweet hot-dipped apples. I would spend mine in town. My heart fluttered, light and happy that morning.

I dragged her past the rise beyond which the train-smoke could no longer be seen. Now miserable Onya dropped her weight and would not carry, would not move another step. I fought for what control I could of our right leg, but this time Onya was the stronger and would not give.

I would not spend my dollar that day.

I was angry but I picked the wildflowers with her on the hill and took them home to Mother.

When we were fifteen, First Mother came to see Mr. Brighton. I pulled Onya back behind a caravan.

First Mother wore a wedding ring now, and her clothes were clean and lovely, ruffled and new. She said she would have us back but Mr. Brighton grew red and waved papers at her and said we would stay.

Onya tried to go to her, but I stopped us. I put my hand over Onya's mouth to keep her from calling out. She bit me deep, but I held silent. I pulled my hand free and slapped her hard. I made us walk among the back tents where we wouldn't be heard while she cried.

First Mother and Mr. Brighton yelled at one another for many hours. She left before sunset, both of them hoarse with the shouting. Sullen Onya would not eat for three days.

When we were sixteen, kind Jacob who watered and fed the horses began to talk to us after shows. One day he laughed too loudly and puffed himself up, waddling like Mr. Brighton. Onya made a sound that must have been a laugh. Jacob touched Onya's cheek as he talked to us. He touched Onya's hair. The man who performed the horses came around the corner as he did this. Mr. Brighton sent for Jacob and we did not see him again after that. Onya cried.

The day we turned seventeen, Mother took our hands to tell news. She smiled, but I felt her trembles. Mr. Brighton had sold our contract to another show.

"You will travel the world," she promised. "You will see Europe. You may see Kings and Emperors!"

I would rather see nothing and stay with Mother, but I was not asked. Onya stood silent. I think she had already begun to plan.

Onya, who would tell *me* to carry our heavy bags—Onya, who never would help with the tents—Onya began holding things for hours. Picking up heavier and heavier things.

She made excuses when I asked why she lifted repeatedly with our right arm. She said she was bored. She said it was nothing. She was playing, she told me. It has been a month now, and determined Onya can carry as much as I.

Three mornings in a row I have awakened to find her already staring at me. This morning, she had already picked up the pillow. I know she will try soon and I am unsure whether I have the will to fight her in this. I am a little envious, in fact.

For the few hours she survives me, she will know what it is to be alone.

Author's note: I've been in relationships where I felt like I couldn't leave. I've seen others in same. I wondered about people who literally COULD NOT LEAVE a relationship. How might that end?

This piece won Gemini magazine's Short Story Contest, 2016. It was nominated for a Pushcart Prize, as well.

PROTECTION

"Damn and blast that Jonah Smithson. This is his doing. Damn him to hell!"

Father, swearing in the barn again.

The words delighted me. I repeated them quietly to myself, practicing for someday. He'd never have gotten away with it if Mother had been near. She'd have stopped him before the second word came out.

I spoke Father's words again, throwing glossy-skinned acorns at Baby Levi's window. It had been *my* window, not long ago.

Lucky for me, Mother was still in town imploring the Most Reverend Charles Taylor to change his mind, go speak with them in the gypsy camp. Them that cursed our town. Ask their forgiveness and see if they wouldn't just move quietly on.

But Reverend Taylor was a coward, cut of the yellowest cloth, and would ask no pardon. He would not apologize for Jonah Smithson's actions. No one would, he declared in loudest tones at the church steps.

Jonah was a God-fearing man, said the Reverend. The heathen woman had stuck her filthy rag-wrapped beggar's hand in his face—and what's more, right after Sunday services. As though the Church hadn't already given her enough.

She earned that slap and maybe more, old Reverend declared.

He was presently on his knees in the church praying down hellfire and brimstone on the gypsies for cursing us.

Mother arrived home in the afternoon. She didn't take Baby Levi down from the carriage. She wouldn't even unhitch Mercy, who protested this with repeated whinnies.

Mother and Father argued some time behind a locked door. I could see through the window— Father waving his arms, reining the anger of his voice, Mother seated—trying to reason, trying to calm him. It rarely worked.

I reached into the buggy and pinched sleeping Levi. His scream ended their argument. I hid behind bushes.

I heard a door-slam and Father stalked to the barn. Mother remained at the table a moment, then left the room. Shortly, I heard her call me.

"'Cilla!" That was strange. Mother wasn't a shouter.

"Priscilla!" she called again.

I ran around to where she now stood by the carriage, nursing Levi back to sleep.

"Get your wraps on. It's cold out."

"Are we going somewhere, Mother?"

"We are, indeed. We are buying protection." Her face was tight and very red. I recognized that look.

Mother had gotten her way.

The wind raged as we neared their camp. Dust blew up, carrying with it the orange and red leaves Mother loved to admire. She ignored them today.

The camp was surrounded by dried brown thistles, protected by thick brambles. Mother made me stay in the carriage, while she called to those inside, begging to be heard out.

I saw long, strong sticks emerge, holding back the bushes and Mother entered. I caught only a glimpse of what seemed to be an enclosed village before the sticks retreated and the thorn-gates snapped shut.

Before an hour had passed, the sticks returned and Mother stepped forth. I strained to see more inside. The rounded door of a gaily decorated cherry-red gypsy wagon was closing, a wrinkled woman on its stoop watching Mother leave. The old woman had a pipe in her teeth and the smoke that rose from it was as blue as a winter lake.

I am not sure why, but I was not surprised when the gypsy woman nodded at me as I stared.

Mother, on the other hand, would not even look my way. She leapt into the carriage, tucking up her long skirts away from the wheels, glanced at the sleeping Levi in the back, and cracked her whip. We dashed homeward.

Or we would have done so, had not a very drunken Jonah Smithson stumbled into the road ahead of us.

"Blast and damn him!" I cried out, Father's words escaping me, betraying me. No sooner was

Mercy stopped than Mother struck me, hard.

I had no time to react. Neither did she. For Jonah Smithson raised a finger to his mouth as though to shush us, but began gnawing on it. His own blood stained the front of his clothes, but he continued to chew his own flesh. A penalty of hands.

The curse was now taking effect, and it seemed fitting that it should start with that very one who brought it down upon us. Soon, it would look this way throughout our town. I shuddered.

Mother ignored me again, whip cracking the air faster and harder above Mercy's head. Mercy frothed, but kept pace.

We did not, as I expected, make for the safety of home. Instead, Mother directed Mercy toward the Smithson house. Mother stopped at the back gate, turning toward me.

"I am going around front to speak to Mrs. Smithson. As I do, you are to go through the back of the house and put Nathaniel Smithson in here." She thrust a burlap sack in my lap.

"Put her baby in a sack?" I couldn't believe she had said it. What had happened inside the gypsy's camp?

"I have bargained for our protection. You need to do as I say and we will never mention this day again. And keep him quiet!" She fairly leaped down from the seat in her haste to be seen consoling Mrs. Smithson for all that had come upon us in recent days.

It was easy enough to make my way in through the house back, as most of the town were out front. There was Nathaniel, as I expected him to be.

I did what I came to do, and as Mother saw me in my seat with the sack, she gestured toward me, telling neighbors she must get me home. They nodded, understanding.

I kept my hand faithfully over that little mouth all the way back to the gypsies. Carried that sack in myself. The gypsy woman took it without a word. She almost smiled at me.

Mother cried all the way home for Nathaniel Smithson. I patted her on her knee.

There was no point in telling her what I'd done. She'd realize it herself soon enough.

Author's note: This piece won first prize at Writers Weekly's Autumn 2014 24-hour contest. As I wrote it, I thought the twist at the end would be that the mother was trading the Smithson's baby for the protection of her own family—terrible enough, right? But toward the end, I realized the little girl had ideas of her own, and I watched in horror...

STIR

Marcus Mason had been an object in motion and had goddamn well intended to *stay* in motion, until he got the wind knocked out of him by an outside force: cancer.

Stage four and pancreatic, no less. His liver and lungs obeyed the ancient laws of hospitality, feeding and housing the cancer as well.

Grateful, it grew.

He resigned the law firm as quietly as he could, convincing them the abdominal pain was a stomach ulcer even worse than the rest of them carried within. They bought it, of course. No one could sell a lie like Marcus. Something compelled him south. Florida. He had been, once, as a young boy. He was convinced the lemons and oranges all over the trees were a joke his parents were playing. And oh, that ocean!

Marcus had run to it, arms outstretched, and let it pound him. It had drawn him into waves like a hug. It drew him now.

Away from the tourist lures he found:

-- ROOMS TO LET --

By week

or month

Marcus almost passed the house indicated by the mailbox-taped sign.

It had all he needed: half-hidden by trees and brush, air conditioners in most windows, and the beach so very near. Seagull-grey shingles, paint peeling, falling off. Bent lightning rod above.

It would do.

He parked at road's edge, careful not to lose too much tire in the sand. As he opened his car door, the humidity welcomed him with a punch. Muscles he had forgotten he had began protesting as he slogged through the deep sand toward the steps.

An   older   man   wearing   Bible-thick

eyeglasses, stained t-shirt, and boxer shorts gave Marcus half a glance and went back to his morning paper.

" 'Morning," Marcus nodded at the man. "This your place?"

The man made no attempt to answer him.

"Sir, do you own this place?" he tried again. "Only, I saw your sign down at the road," he gestured behind him but the man wouldn't acknowledge.

"Oh!" A woman's voice from within. "I thought I heard a car stop." Her slippers masked her footfalls as she quickly appeared in a too-brightly flowered housecoat. She eyed him through the screen silently, blowing smoke. Her voice told Marcus that cigarette never left the left corner of her mouth.

"You're awful young to be—"she began and stopped herself. " 'Course, we get all kinds—"

"Mercy." The newspaper man interrupted. "Send 'im on his way." He flipped to the sports section, never looking up.

Mercy's mouth hardened visibly and she drew on a tight smile.

"Excuse me, Dave Williams, I suppose *you* pay the mortgage around here?" She turned back to

Marcus. "How long would you need the room?"

Marcus hadn't considered this. "Umm," he shrugged. "Couple weeks, maybe?"

"Well, where are you headed? Not much further south you can go." She picked a piece of tobacco off her tongue.

"Not really headed anywhere. I just wanted somewhere quiet. Do a little fishing."

"Uh-huh." Silence.

"Listen, if this is a problem, I'll just keep looking. I need a place. Doesn't have to be here."

She tossed a defiant look at Dave Williams. "Yeah, I got a room for you. Go get your bags."

Newspaper Man hawked and spat his disapproval off the side of the porch.

"MIND THE LINE"

Someone had stenciled the warning over the kitchen doorway. Marcus imagined a houseful of senior citizens raising canes and walkers at one another, fighting to receive the biggest spoonful of creamed corn.

"Rent's $200 a week," the woman had been speaking to him. "You don't look like that'll break you none."

"No, that's fine. That's fine," Marcus was half-listening, only half-caring. The house was quiet but for a distant television. That was good enough for him. "How many people you got here?"

She ignored his question, continuing with her script. "I'd like that $200 in cash, beginning of the week. You'll share a bathroom with three other men—you watch out for Harley, now. He'll walk in on you in the tub, fine-lookin' young man like yourself. I'll show you how to wedge the door shut from 'im."

She pointed out Marcus's seat and he took it. From one of the cabinets, she pulled out a mimeographed contract for the room, all the while detailing the dos and don'ts of living in her house. The lawyer living in Marcus's brain rose to attention. He talked it back down.

She handed him a pen and he signed, pulling out a wallet thick with twenties. He handed her ten of them.

Upstairs, he threw his bags on his bed, propped open all three windows, and let the ocean sing him to sleep. Marcus was up at sunrise. The blessed hands of Mercy Porter were frying bacon and coffee was waiting for him.

Last night, he had dreamt of fishing, standing knee-high in those waves for hours. Mercy found him an old pole at the house while warning him not to go too deep in. "Drop-off out there. You can't see it. Stay far away from them tall rocks and you'll be fine."

She had packed his lunch, adding several bottles of beer in the cooler. She told him it was an investment. He owed her fish for dinner. He made a mental note to tip Mercy well when he left.

He took his time walking up to the shore. Breathing wasn't coming easy to him.

It was good to be alone at the beach. The rocks Mercy warned him about recalled to him the stories of standing stones in Europe. A little Stonehenge.

He sat when he needed to regain strength, and the pulsed heartbeat of wave-rhythm gave him the most peace he'd known since his diagnosis. A couple and their dog were up-coast far enough that he could hear the dog's barking, but no one came closer than that.

Marcus pulled eight fine sheepshead from the waters that day.

Mercy' voice gruffed when she saw them. "Haven't had sheepshead since Mr. Porter was alive. He'd bring 'em home every Saturday."

Marcus cleaned them under the back porch and brought them in for frying while he bathed.

The dinnerbell warned everyone to queue up. Most of the men were already near, drawn by the scent-link of pan-seared fish to their memories. Mercy called Marcus up to the front to be first-served.

"Oh, no, you don't," Marcus laughed. "I saw the sign." He gestured behind him above the doorway.

Mercy seemed genuinely confused.

"The words?" He decided to explain the joke: "You know, 'Mind the line'? Don't want to get in trouble with anyone."

Understanding dawned on her. "Ah, right. No, that's just..." Her voice trailed off and she shrugged. "Well, here it is. You like lemon? Butter? You wait for grace, now."

One by one, men in various degrees of disrepair began filing in to chairs. Some of them balanced their own plates, shuffling slowly; others waited as Mercy set their food before them.

When all were seated, Mercy took the head of the table and bowed them.

"O Lord, we thank Thee for Thy bounty and for what Thou has put before us."

"Amen," the men chorused. Marcus sat silently.

He squeezed lemon on his plate and scooped a bite of fish.

Five a.m. brought clear warm skies and Marcus made up his mind to fill Mercy's freezer with what he caught. Something to remember him by when he was gone. Pole, bucket, and cooler and by five-thirty, he was off.

After an hour of meditation in the waves, Marcus caught a dark dot moving toward him. The dot revealed itself to be Dave Williams, sans newspaper.

Dave stood back a ways from Marcus, watching, never speaking, not even when a coughing fit wracked Marcus. After a bit, he turned and walked back the way he had come. Close to lunchtime, Dave appeared again, this time carrying his own rod and bucket.

The two men fished, silently, popping beers until the sun said it was time to head home. Dave dumped his catch into Marcus' bucket and rinsed his hands at the fish table. "Gonna sit a while before dinner," were his first words to Marcus that day.

Marcus cleaned the fish and took them into Mercy. She patted his cheek.

The week passed quickly. Marcus passed Mercy another $200 without a word and she nodded, understanding. Every day, Marcus came back sooner from the shore. Fewer fish, but the freezer was already bursting. He found peace out there. Still, the sun warned him he was giving in earlier every day.

By the middle of Marcus' third week, Dave began walking out to the strand *with* Marcus instead of catching him up later. A small exchange played between them, always on the topic of fishing. Until one day it wasn't.

"Marcus Mason," Dave spoke with a sigh that held gravity.

Marcus looked at the man, squinting between clouds.

"Way I see it," Dave continued, "you are much too young to be retired. What are you, twenty-five?"

Marcus answered wryly. "Thirty-three next month." He'd begun dragging an old aluminum-framed chair out to the shore these days. He sat in it now, rod secured in the sand holder. He had a good idea where the conversation was headed.

"Thirty-three," Dave repeated, examining Marcus to confirm the number. He nodded. "Well, your Benz tells me you've got some money. However you made it, you don't seem in a hurry to get back to that life."

"Pole dancing. You had a look at my ass?"

Dave laughed. "No such thing. Mercy Googled you already. Junior partner, Coneelly, Engels, and Engels. You were doing okay."

It was a question rather than a statement, but Marcus answered it with a shrug and popped a beer.

He drank all of it before answering.

"Ulcers." The lie was sour on his own tongue. Or so he thought.

Marcus bent double and retched in the sand. It was a new symptom, somewhere on the list the doctor gave him at the end of their argument. He lost his breath and began coughing. He was surprised at how much blood he expelled.

Dave saw it all. "Ulcers, huh? You think I don't hear you wheezing every step out here, every morning?"

"Listen, I—"

"You're turning *grey*, boy."

Marcus picked himself up into his seat, finally looking Dave full-on.

"Pancreatic, stage four. Liver and lungs, too," Marcus finally admitted. It actually felt good to get that out.

Dave nodded. "Yeah, I thought it was something like that. No Chemo? Radiation?"

Marcus shook his head, spat a bitter laugh. "For what? To draw it out a little longer? Nah. I don't have kids. Not married. No. Game over. I'm going out fishing. And enjoying your company." He snorted.

They said no more on the matter. At the usual hour, Dave began packing up both his things and Marcus' for the trip back to the house.

"Leave it," Marcus gestured at his items. "I'm gonna stay out a whil--" As he finished speaking, he was bent double in the sand again.

Dave waited for it to pass, then helped Marcus up. Dave draped Marcus' arm around his own shoulders and the two headed home.

Mercy herself had taken up Dave's seat on the porch. They arrived just as she was finishing one cigarette and starting another. Marcus was exhausted, but not so much that he didn't notice the look pass between the two: Dave gave Mercy a double nod and she, in turn, raised an eyebrow at him.

Mercy came down from the porch and

together two septuagenarians got the young lawyer into his own bed.

And Marcus slept.

Late morning, two days later, Marcus' body granted him a reprieve and he headed back to the shoreline. Dave was already there, among the rocks Mercy warned about.

Dave saw him approaching and sent him a wave and half-smile.

"Gonna want to be careful, there," Marcus cautioned. "Bottom drops out and the tide'll get you. Mercy heard stories, I guess."

"Yep. Know all about the rocks, but thank you."

Dave stretched his hand toward Marcus to help steady him in the shifts of sand.

They moved to their usual spot. The winds seemed calmer today.

"You have family we need to know about?" Dave handed Marcus a beer. "If something should happen, that is?"

"Don't want to get stuck with the body,

huh?" Marcus managed a smile.

"Naw. That's not it. Pretty much all of us have faced the idea. Harley's probably the youngest at the house, least until you showed up. He's sixty-eight. And Mercy has had to call 9-1-1 for a few while I've been here.

"No," he continued. "But if we needed to let anyone know..." He trailed off and let Marcus put two and two together.

"Like I said, never married. Never reproduced. Parents gone." Marcus shrugged. "Just me."

"Sorry to hear that." Dave's voice had dropped by an octave.

After a moment, Dave offered, "You're in the right place, you know."

"Yeah, it's beautiful down here. I thought about Hawaii. Just didn't seem right. I came down here with my parents. Good trip, good trip. Maybe that's why I headed this way? Be near them, somehow?"

"Not what I meant," Dave told him. "Maybe you're supposed to be here. At the house. Everyone of us has somethin' going on like that," here he gestured at Marcus's abdomen. "We've all had the hourglass tipped over.

"Sand running out one way or another..." His voice trailed off into the oncoming tide.

"You?" Marcus asked.

"Bones."

"You getting treatment?"

"Remission. Creeping back up on me, though. Gonna need something real soon."

Marcus nodded at him. A couple pelicans were debating fishing rights a few hundred feet out into the water.

"This the place to come, then? Terminally ill drawn like lemmings to the waters edge. Literally." He smiled at his own joke.

Dave was staring at him. He started to say something just as Marcus's fishing rod took a hard hit.

"I think I should tell you--Ha HA! WHOA! Grab 'im boy! Play it out. Play it out. Bring him to you."

Marcus's rod curled into a hard C, his arm tensed and screaming from the effort it took to wind line.

Dave was whooping it up behind him, cheering him as the fish finally broke the surface.

"Well, I'll be! That is a beautiful snook! Just look at it!"

Dave ran into the waves with the net and brought back Marcus's prize. He slapped Marcus's back as he handed it over like an award.

"Well, that's easily worth another beer," Dave insisted.

"None for me," Marcus collapsed into his chair, winded and laughing. Then he bent and retched and his world turned black. There was whispering, an argument, in the hallway. It had invaded his dreams disguised as dune grasses scratching the wind. He swam to the surface and woke up. He was in his room with no idea how he got there.

The back deck was littered with Adirondack-style chairs, and Marcus dropped into one near Dave, sighing.

"You don't have to die of this thing, Marcus."

"Yeah. I do, actually. What do you mean, chemo? I don't want a couple more months, Dave. Not months like that."

"Not what I meant." Dave shifted in his seat. "Not what I meant at all."

The older man bit a hangnail and spat it out to sand.

"*Hope,*" he explained.

Marcus laughed. "Hope? Jesus! I thought for a minute you were importing pills from Mexico or Europe or something. Oh, God, it hurts to laugh. Hope," he snorted.

"You done?" Dave asked, eyebrows raised.

"Ah, sure. Go get me a beer and tell me all about how hope is going to save me."

"Hope saves. I've seen it happen." Dave nodded to himself. "You're here for a reason, Marcus. This place, this time, this house—all for a reason.

"Those tall rocks out in the ocean. Mercy told you to keep out of them—and she was right to say that. Because there's something powerful in 'em, Marcus. Aw, hell, you laugh if you want, but I have *seen* it, Marcus."

Marcus leaned his head back in his chair and closed his eyes. Dave continued.

"How well you know your Bible stories, boy? Your Mama take you to Sunday School?

Hell, yeah, she did. You remember the Pool of Bethesda?"

"Ah, no. Guess Mom missed that week." Marcus kept his eyes shut.

"It was a pool of water where the sheep drank. And an angel of the Lord would descend and stir up those waters and who ever made it in first would be healed of whatever afflicted them. Jesus healed a guy who couldn't make it in in time. Others always pushed past him to get in, get their healing. They didn't mind the line, those days."

Something clicked. Marcus's eyes snapped open. " 'Mind the line'?" He emphasized each word, almost in anger. "You're bullshitting me. That's what that means—over the kitchen? 'Mind the Line' means stay out of—what, the rocks? The ocean rocks?—until it's your turn? Sweet Jesus, Dave. You can't be serious. Look at you. You're sitting there like you're actually serious."

"Keep it down, boy. Keep it down. I told you, I have *seen it happen*."

Dave kept his eyes toward the far ocean. "I wasn't just out there to fish with you. Even if you hadn't been out there every day, I'd have gone to check the waters. Been building lately. Longer between each time. We might lose it entirely at some point."

"So, whose turn is it? Yours, I guess, or you

wouldn't be out there every day."

Dave didn't answer.

"Yeah, yeah, it's your turn," Marcus scoffing turned to bitterness. "Not nice to make fun of the terminally ill, man. Pretty shitty joke, actually."

Marcus stood to go, but Dave held up a hand to stop him.

"I want to make you a deal. A trade."

"What do you want from me, Dave?"

"Obvious, isn't it?" The old man's face reddened. "I'll trade you my turn for money. *Buy my healing.* Hell, go back to your law office and make it all back again in a year. I get some money to live out the rest of my days somewhere better than this shack. Maybe get a girlfriend. What good is a healing to me? What good is another ten, twenty years as an old man? It doesn't heal *age.*"

"What's to keep me from just going out there and taking your turn anyway?"

"I'm willing to bet you can't make it out there on your own again. You need my help."

Dave had called his bluff.

Marcus let the screen door slam as he went to his room. Mercy loaded his plate with scrambled eggs. There was no talk of a day of fishing ahead any longer.

"Thank you, Mercy," Marcus said quietly as she placed his plate on the table for him. They had the dining room to themselves.

"What Dave said to you last night," Mercy took a long sip of orange juice before continuing. "It's true. You didn't wonder why there's a houseful of old people about ten miles from anything?"

Marcus didn't know what to think. So Mercy was in on it, too.

"Guess I thought you all knew each other. Thought you collected them. Like strays. Crazy cat lady, but no cats." He looked at his breakfast while he spoke.

"They ended up here the same way as you ended up here. Meant to be." She tipped the last of her bacon onto his plate.

"Here," she told him. "Too damn skinny."

Marcus found Dave reading the newspaper on the front porch, looking very much like he did the first day Marcus arrived.

"So, how do I do this? Do I write you a

check? Go to the bank? I'll transfer to your account."

"You believe me, then?" Dave asked over the top of the sports section. "It's important that you believe. I think your hope is half the magic of it."

Marcus shrugged. "I'm not sure I care any more. I'm on my way out, I figure. You fished with me. Helped me when I was sick. We shared more than a few beers. Money's gotta go somewhere. I want Mercy to get some of it, too."

Dave didn't answer that. "I was up along the shoreline this morning. Wouldn't surprise me if it's churning by this evening. That's what we're looking for. Turmoil in the water. Whirlpool. It oughta look like it's being stirred."

Turmoil in the water. Marcus rolled his eyes. *For crying out loud.*

He went back into the house to start cutting checks. Mercy slapped fresh bedlinens on Marcus's dresser. "Mr. Porter was the first I ever saw. Dave—you think he's feeding you a line. But, nope. It is a sight to behold. A few of us from the house are gonna come up tonight and have a watch, if you don't mind."

"What happened to Mr. Porter?"

"Car accident a few years back. But they

were good years we had together. The best."

Dave. Now, he could believe Dave would bullshit him. But he couldn't shake the conviction he saw on Mercy's face. That was real.

She believed it.

Dinnertime was nearing. Marcus had no appetite. He had handed checks over to both Mercy and Dave earlier. Mercy had actually kissed his cheek.

Marcus saw Dave headed out to the beach shortly after he heard plates cleared below. It wasn't long before Dave came jogging back.

"Time!" He burst into Marcus's room. "It's time!"

Marcus tried to hide his disappointment. He had hoped to end the charade after distributing his checks, maybe get more rest. He suspected it wouldn't be much longer for him now.

But they were determined to play it out. Marcus went along. The water was restless—that much was clear from a distance. Marcus caught Dave in a little dance at one point as they approached the shore. Dave believed. That was clear.

Mercy had tagged along, as had Charlie, John, and Al. A tug in Marcus's chest told him that Al wouldn't have wrestled his walker out here onto sand for no reason. The skeptic in Marcus gave way by another inch or so.

The water inside the rocks swirled. It rose and fell, but never left the border of rocks. Marcus was transfixed. Dave caught his arm.

"Marcus, do you believe? Even a bit?"

"Maybe," Marcus began. "Yeah, maybe a bit. Let's do this." He stepped between the rocks and allowed the waters to take him.

Heat, electricity spiked through him. His spine, abdomen, neck all knew fire. The cancer was being consumed, he told himself. Here he opened his eyes.

Dave had his hands wide, one on each rock either side of him. His eyes were closed and he was shaking.

Mercy and the other three men were behind him. Charlie took a step forward only to be slapped by Mercy. "Mind the line!" she snarled. "It's Dave's turn."

Marcus wanted to correct her, to laugh, "No, it's *my* turn," but he found it harder to breathe, to stand. He began to notice a kind of heat wave coming forth from him and making its way to the circle's edge. Toward Dave.

"But it's *my* turn," Marcus tried to protest. The words never came.

The old man opened his mouth and breathed deeply, sucking in whatever came from Marcus. Mercy smiled. "You've got 'im, Dave. You got 'im. Just a little bit more."

Dave nodded, hands still riding the rocks, already looking stronger.

Marcus' knees buckled at this point. He drained quickly and was shredded by the remains of the stir.

Author's note: That story in the Bible messed me up. It wasn't Jesus doing a miracle, but some crazy wild water stirred by an angel, so the people said. I still wonder what was going on back then. This piece won 2nd place at the Westmoreland County Arts and Heritage Festival, and then 4th place at Five-on-the-Fifth's Autumn 2016 short story competition.

TAP

"Do you hear it?"

Gran turns to me, like a child waking, unsure.

I take her hearing aids, change the batteries. They must be whistling in her ears again. I tell her it's the wind, pat her lap-lain hands, tense and gnarled. Summer storms due all day, I say.

New calves and mothers begin the slow shift toward the woods and shelter. The pond's bounty of cattails struggle to remain upright. I turn to hand back the hearing aids and see the wisps again.

It isn't a spider's web swaying in the corner of Gran's picture window, but every time I look to the lower farm, the threads catch my eye. I move to look closer while Gran is up, pushing her walker kitchenward, to steam the spring's last asparagus.

It is a silken fairy shell snagged on windowsill splinters, visible now where farmdust clings to it to tell her story: she'd been caught and pulled, stretched out by her long arms—a tug of war the winds finally won. Her wings tangled and shredded, head bowed like a crucifix, toes pointed toward an earth they would never again touch.

I lose time watching her strands rise and fall, counting her silent taps on glass. Gran works her way back into the room: "Don't you hear it?" she insists again.

I still hear nothing.

"Oh, but you must," she tilts her head at me. "Someone keeps knocking. "

Author's note: This piece won third prize at PennWriters one-day conference in Erie, Pa. Based on something I saw in my Grandmother's window. Should have taken a photo.

CHURN

Walking. The man had walked most of the night, pausing only occasionally to cough, hawk, and spit. He might pass a willow soon, cut some bark to chew to relieve his sore throat. Still he trudged on, following the stream. Rain began to pelt the dirt, drops shattering like mirrorglass, like spidersacs dropped and burst open to reveal a thousand within.

At a crossroads ahead, a young girl played beneath an enormous oak, digging a small branch into the earth and flicking it upward toward the tree's trunk. Now and then, she would spin around to flare her long dress, purple-crimson-purple. As he neared, he saw they were toadstools she was gouging and flicking. A large circle of red-spotted toadstools at the base of an oak. Fairy-ring, they called that when he was young.

She was chanting something he never got to hear, for one vigorous flick made her lose her balance on the rain-slicked mossy roots below her and she landed on her backside.

"Here!" he called, "I've got you."

He rushed forward to help, but she was up in a flash. Her scarf had come loose and out tumbled strands of web-white hair. She quickly tucked it back up and brushed herself off.

"The faeries done it," she explained her fall. "Mam says I mustn't disturb them."

"You've not hurt yourself, then?" he asked.

"Oh, no," she assured him. "They do it all the time." She paused, eyeing his satchel. "Are you supposed to be here?"

Her look told him she was quite sure he shouldn't be.

"You ought not stand there, you know." She pointed at several cut ropes above her. "You're beneath a hanging tree. That will bring bad luck if you're traveling."

Ignoring her omen, he sat beneath the tree, loosened his shoes for a needed rest. He asked, nodding at the ropes, "What was that about, then?"

She hesitated. "I wasn't there for it. Mam made me stay home. She never lets me go." Her voice held a slight trace of sulk.

"You're out here now, though." He ran a hand through his hair, picked at the long grasses, and looked around. "Your Mam, she lets you play at the hanging tree?"

"Nobody hanging today," she shrugged. "And anyway, Mam wants me to wait for the churn."

"Someone is bringing you a churn, out here?" It seemed an unlikely place to meet, but he couldn't remember small village ways.

She laughed at him. "No. The *churn*. The ground-churn. She wants me to wait for them to come back." She began poking toadstools again.

"Who is coming back?" His heart began pounding, hard, in his throat. He coughed. Perhaps more were being hanged today. Not his business, not really something he wanted to see.

"Them as was hanged. Sometimes it takes days. Could be weeks, even, Mam said. Bit of a time-muddle. But the rain will bring them back up again. She'll get them, all the same."

Flick. Flick.

He didn't want to ask the question, but found

himself doing it. "Why does she want them?"

She pointed where willow trees thick-lined the bank, brookside. Their long branches combed through the waters like nets. "She needs to make more willows to help find the lost babe below. Mam won't stop until our babe is found." There was a pride in her voice. She added, as an after-thought, "He was a seventh-son. That's why they drowned him. They were afraid. But Mam knows them who did it. Getting them takes time, is all." She smiled.

It hadn't been much of a rest. The traveler thought perhaps it was a choice moment to be moving along. He tied his shoes tightly, telling the girl, "I will leave you to your work and waiting, then. You sound quite certain they'll come back."

"Well, *you* did." She wrapped her arms across herself, smug. "Don't you even know who you are?"

He tried to rise. It hadn't occurred to him to wonder before who he was. It hadn't seemed to matter. Walking had been all that was important. He found now he was unable to stand.

"Ah, no point in getting' up. You're on fae ground. They'll hold you here now for Mam. You came back so quickly. I wasn't sure. I'll let her know you're back." She turned and ran.

Her words hovered, lost in a hot flood of

thought and images: a silent crowd of hooded men--he had been among them--carrying the stolen newborn to the creek, plunging the child into its icy heart, the anxious shouts of many men, and later, hands laid upon him and the cut and twist of rope on his neck.

Author's note: This piece won first place in Brilliant Flash Fiction's Second Anniversary writing contest. I do love me some creepy children and malevolent fae.

REMISSION

Captain Jaeger of the trawler *Dogger* gave orders that the search should continue through the night. He himself often slept on the bridge, starting awake at every sound, every noise. He snapped at his men more often these days...

Aggie knew the slobbering pack wasn't far behind her and Jimmy Marcusson himself was in the lead. Jimmy didn't often come to do his own dirty work. This thought made fourteen-year-old Aggie Andrews run harder.

She slipped on the slimy toadstools that grew thick under the evergreens lining the island's hills.

She took a kneeful of pine needles, but decided to let that pain register later.

At the edge of the pines, Aggie leapt over a chunk of boulder, dropping fifteen feet below where the barest patch of soft sand caught her. This looked like a daring act of insanity, but it was quite grounded in reason. She was an island girl and this was *her* territory. Jimmy spent his days in town. He didn't know this end of the island like she did. All he would see were sharp gashes of rock, the ocean just beyond. She tucked under the boulder's jutting edge, held tight to a small lip of sandstone.

"Holy Mother of God—she killed herself!"

"Did you see that? That was insane!"

"That did NOT just happen."

"Jesus—that has to be a hundred feet straight down!"

Aggie could hear them wheezing. She focused all her control on breathing silently while her body begged the right to hurl. Concentrating hard on the far-off trawler, she half-hoped someone on it would notice the pack and put an end to the pursuit.

The just-past-puberty voice of Jimmy Marcusson broke through: "Listen to me. LISTEN." All other sounds ceased.

"We go back into town and pick up a game of football in Stanson's field. That's where we've been all morning. You got it? All morning."

The only person that dared speak back to Jimmy was his sister, Ginny.

"But, Jimmy. It was an accident. It ain't like you pushed her."

Jimmy countered fast and hard: "You want Mom and Dad to go to jail, Ginny? Because that's what'll happen if you say anything. Someone always goes to jail, and we're minors so it won't be us. They'll take Mom and Dad."

Ginny started wailing, but stopped with a punch from Jimmy. "Shut up. We gotta get back."

The shuffling of their feet told Aggie they'd gone. Cautious, Aggie began counting one thousand waves crashing into the foot of the abandoned lighthouse far to her left. Aggie long ignored its "No Trespassing" sign. She had spent many days curled up reading in the haven base of it, undisturbed.

Her thousand-count complete, she picked her way carefully toward her lighthouse. Here on the crags that held back the sea, slippery algae could end your life even faster than Jimmy Marcusson and company.

She was twenty yards from the light when

she saw him. He resembled the pile of laundry that lay strewn, ever-present, across her bedroom floor. But this particular pile of laundry had a very discernible head. Seagulls, like sky-sharks, circled above.

"Hey!" she called at the heap. A seagull landed on the mound and began to peck at the clothing. No response.

No ship was nearby, save the creaking trawler that had passed earlier. It had shown no panicked signs of having had a man overboard.

Aggie grabbed a long stick the tides had pushed among the stones and approached the pile. The seagull shot her a reproachful look and abandoned its claim. She nudged him with the stick, wedged it under his body, and flipped him onto his back.

"Mister. Hey, *mister*." The skin of his thick-brown bearded face was almost grey. She touched it with the back of her hand. Cold. But a whisper of warmth underneath.

"Exposure can kill a man faster than dehydration," she had heard. And this man was certainly exposed, half in the early spring ocean, half out.

Running for help would have to wait. He didn't look like he had the time it would take to go and return. And getting help would mean admitting she had trespassed.

A quick glance found another stick equal to her first. Inside the lighthouse were a couple ratty blankets the previous keeper left, thin enough to tie easily. She did this, creating a make-shift stretcher she lay next to the man. Lifting him was out of the question. She rolled him onto it, picked up two ends and dragged him out of the water as best she could toward the only shelter available.

Inside the base of the light was the nest Aggie had created. She tossed aside her books, lay the stretcher next to the mattress she'd salvaged from the keeper's house and rolled the man that way.

She untied the stretcher, layered the blankets over him, scanning him for signs of life. Her canteen lay nearby and, pulling back his massed tangle of hair, she tipped a cap full into his pried-open mouth. The barest of sounds came forth. But Aggie knew it was a *good* sound. She continued tipping one cap at a time until at last he gave a quiet sigh that she took to mean he had his fill. His eyes remained closed.

She leaned back against the inner brick wall of the lighthouse wondering whether she could fetch food. The incoming tide answered that question. The light was isolated by the encroaching waters through the day. The old road that once connected had long since washed away. They would be cut off for several hours, now, at least. Aggie scavenged in the old backpack she kept under the stairs, hoping for some proper sustenance. Gum, beef jerky, a stale pack of crackers. Useless.

She pulled her knees up close underneath her sweater and shut her eyes for a bit, thinking.

She was startled from her sleep by a whispered "thank you" coming from the blankets just a few feet away. She righted herself, crawled over to him. His eyes were barely open. She touched his face. No longer pale cold, instead it was burning and glowing a wet red. Infection. He needed more water. And proper food.

He began to shake with chills. "Filthy," she thought he said.

Aggie carefully gave him what was left of the water in her canteen, told him she had to go, but wouldn't be long. It wasn't true. Her own house was closest—still over half an hour away—and it was almost that amount again to the next. She grabbed her backpack.

By now, the waters had receded over the road. She was used to soggy sneakers and half-walked, half-ran, squelching, home. Aggie got her wish: Gran wasn't home. She loaded up on what food and water might not be missed.

The man had cast off his blankets when she arrived back at the light. She tilted his head up, making him sip a full bottle of water before allowing him to lie back down. She took his hand. Cooler. The fever had passed.

"I wish I knew what to do for you."

He gave her hand a gentle squeeze.

There was more moonlight than sun in the sky when she decided to head home. She left water bottles by the man with a promise to return at first light.

He was sitting at an angle when she arrived just after dawn. His full-face smile was gentle and slow.

"I wondered if I had dreamed you," he told her. He slid down the wall to one side and slept. She cleaned his garments in ocean water.

Late that afternoon, she found him looking at her. Her face warmed. She felt shy and wondered why. "Did you find the food I left? Was there enough water? I brought you more."

He nodded. "I had some bites of the sandwich. It was delicious. Thank you." His eyes were dark like the night ocean. Her throat tightened.

"Can you stand?"

"Not well. I tried earlier. Still dizzy. I think I hit my head, but can't remember where. Or when."

"I'm Aggie. Agatha. Who are you?"

He tried to smile while shaking his head. "Sorry. I can't remember that, either."

"No matter. You're on Pine Island," she offered. "Is that where you're supposed to be?"

"I don't know. Island?" He thought. "No. I remember water. I was fighting my way through so much of it. Like it would never end." He shrugged. "I woke up in here with just you and this headache for company."

Aggie opened her backpack. "I brought lots of tape and bandages for you. And here," she handed him a brown bottle. "You're going to want this on those cuts. You were worried about how dirty you were. I tried to clean you." She reddened.

Now he was awake and sitting up, he looked

younger to Aggie than he did as a heap. His hair and beard were the quiet brown of driftwood. She caught her hand reaching to touch it.

"You know, I ache everywhere. Absolutely everywhere, but at the same time, I feel wonderful." He dared a small laugh. "Maybe that's what happens when you're hit on the head."

"How can you feel wonderful?"

"It's like...I'm feeling breezes on my skin for the first time. It's like the wind is silk and velvet. This cold floor—here—" He took Aggie's hand and placed it on the cement. "I feel every stone, every grain of sand. It's magnificent." He had tears beginning. "And do you smell what's in the air?" He tilted his head back, closing his eyes. "Salt. It stings my nose." He laughed one note. "Fish. Seaweed warmed by sun. Pine sap flowing. Do you *smell* it, Aggie?"

His face glowed in the coming dusk. Aggie nodded, unable to look away from him.

"The sound of waves. Like a broom across gravel. An old woman sweeping up the shore." He paused, looked her full-on. Her stomach clenched. "I want to go outside. Do you think you can help me walk? I want to see it, feel it. I want *sun*."

"Here." She stood and put one arm under his, helping him to his feet. She tucked herself under one side of him to help balance. His arm slipped from her shoulder, unable to hold. He slumped to the floor.

"Not ready yet, I think." He pulled himself back to his blankets. "Another day, maybe."

"Or a week," Aggie cautioned. "You need to eat more. Drink more." She opened her backpack, let him take what he wanted. "What else can I bring?"

"You've done so much already. Please. This is perfect."

"Do you want me to get help?"

"Help? What help would I need? Look at all you've done. I'm mending."

They regarded one another for a moment.

"Here's something: I wish I could get clean. I can feel something all over me. I'm filthy. When I'm able to get up, will you help me to the water?"

"I kept you as clean as I could when you were sleeping. When you couldn't wake up."

"I know. I know what you did, and I thank you for it. This is different though." His face said he was casting about in his mind for just the right way to describe it. "It's like there's *grease* over me. I don't feel like myself. I feel wrong."

"It'll pass," she assured him. "Gran says we feel like different people when we've been sick."

"Yes. I suppose that's so. Still, I'm looking forward to a wash." He yawned. "I'll sleep some more now."

"I need to be going, anyway. Gran will worry. It's too many late nights."

His eyes were already closed.

"Please be okay," she prayed as her feet selected a safe path back to the island.

When Aggie arrived on the third day, she was surprised to see on the floor an elaborate seahorse, seastars, a jellyfish, all from shells and sand, arranged in spiral beauty. The man grinned at her, sheepish, from near the rounded staircase. He held one of the sleek small mice that frequented the building, stroking its head. He knelt down and released it.

"I was up early," he shrugged. He took Aggie's hand and led her carefully between the designs to where she could see better.

Aggie couldn't speak. She had never seen anything like it.

"Thank you for all you've done for me, Aggie. I feel a thousand times better."

"You look cleaner. Were you in the water already?"

"I was," he sighed. "It didn't help. I'm letting that go. I'm restless. Got to keep moving."

Aggie wouldn't look at him. "You're leaving then," her eyes on the adorned floor. The man reached over and tipped up her chin. She looked up, unwilling.

"You ever go up?" He nodded up at the light.

"Yeah. All the time," she answered grudgingly. "I read up there."

"May I see it?" He was shining at Aggie. "I was still shaky this morning. Thought I'd wait on you."

The ascending took strength from him. Aggie secretly hoped the stress would convince him to stay longer, but at the top much of his energy returned. He stepped from the doorway, catching the rail with a gasp. Aggie wasn't surprised by this. Every time she emerged from the stairs she caught her own breath.

Teal, turquoise, cerulean, indigo, cobalt, ultramarine. The ocean was at once all of these and none of them. It defied categorization.

He grabbed for her hand, squeezing but not hard. "Don't know if I like it up here," he began. "Maybe I fell once. Fell. Could that be how I hurt my head? No, I don't think it was that..." He spoke more to himself than to Aggie. His face whitened. Aggie knew a trick to get his mind off the height.

"Watch this," she told him and she leaned back into the doorway and grabbed a stone from the pile she kept, hurled it as far as she could. The splash was indiscernible. "Couldn't you just stay here?"

"Got to keep moving. That's the strongest idea in me now. But you're right—all this beauty around us—and I look at you. And I want to *cry* for your beauty. No," he shook his head. "Don't worry. It's not like that. It's different. Deeper."

"Beautiful? No one ever called me beautiful." She spoke what had been on her mind the past three days. "Beautiful is what *you* are. You must be perfect. I could look at you forever." She joked, "I could almost bow down in front of you."

His face froze at these words. Confusion swept over his features. He bent double like a stab, reaching for her and pushing her away at the same time.

Aggie thought he might heave and stepped back. "Are you okay?"

A whisper retched forth from him: "All this I will give You if You bow down and worship me." The man fell to his knees and then forward, his head pressed to the cement.

"What?" Aggie cried out, fearing he might roll between the bars, off the edge. She moved toward him. He began to convulse.

"No!" he screamed at her. "Go, Aggie. Get away! It's back! I remember everything! GO!"

Once it began, it happened quickly. His voice spewed anger and stench. It promised pain. He was no longer beautiful.

She turned, fled down the inside steps, addled from both the turn of the stairs and forgetting to breathe. He pursued.

Aggie made for the door, but tripped over a stray blanket. She caught herself but it slowed her. He caught her, whipped her around in a pivot to face him. He bore little resemblance now to what he had been. What she was able to recognize made it worse. He grabbed her throat, began to squeeze.

"Marcusson," he snarled. "*Where?*" His leaned, his face now inches from her own, daring her to lie.

Her insides seized. Jimmy Marcusson? She hesitated. He noticed, sneering.

"You want him gone, too."

"No," she protested.

Hearing her own voice made her bolder. A storm tightened her insides. She blasted her answer at him, raged at what he had done to her friend. The friend she saved from infection. The friend who patterned seashells to see her delight. The friend who had shut his eyes, drunk on the beauty of this world.

"NO!"

Nothing mattered anymore. Let him claim *her* if he must. But he wasn't going to take anyone else. She would see to that. Every cell in her body burned in anger and loss. She pressed toward him to show that she, too, could be horrible. "NO." Aggie seethed, daring him to defy her. He took a step backwards.

From the water, a horn blared with such power Aggie was knocked to the ground. He twisted away from the sound, leaping boulders until he reached the edge of the island and dove in. She did not see him surface. Sometime later it occurred to her that he might not need to.

Aggie went in to the base of the light to clean up. She cried but kept working. She thought, as she cleaned, about the trawler's blast. It had, of course, never crossed her mind to wonder what they had been trawling for.

Captain Jaeger slumped into his chair, letting out a full-body sigh. He brushed his hand over his grizzled chin, wiped grains from his eyes. They had been close. Might have had him, even, but it had been more important to scare him off from the girl.

There would be other opportunities.

Author's note: Oh, how I adore Aggie! I loved her so much, that I made her the female lead in my still-not-finished YA novel. But, I digress. There's a Bible verse that says Satan prowls the earth, seeking whom he may devour. This piece takes that literally, and couples it with the question: if Satan had a hard enough knock on the head, might he forget he was evil? This piece took 2nd place in 2014 at Writers Type's 3rd Quarter contest.

ISLAND TALE

You were asking me about that island earlier, Will, the one that looks like it's got a kids' rope-swing hanging out over it on one end? Naw, kids don't go out there anymore. They used to, long time ago. Used to dare each other after it happened. Guess you should know about the whole thing, now you and your Amy are taking over your granddad's farm. I'm surprised he ain't never told you this.

Here's another beer. Want anything stronger? No? Huh. You might, before I'm done.

Guess it started in the late 1780's or so. A young man, Moyers, itching with a fresh law degree in his hand purchased himself an island smack dab in the center of the Allegheny River.

The Indians had called it "Darkness," from all those trees, and it's just up north of here in front of Riverdale, proper.

Man built himself either a house or beaver dam. All the farmers and fishermen snickered when it was mentioned. But he musta built it better than they gave him credit for, because he lived there through some of Western Pennsylvania's toughest snow storms and come springtime when he'd show himself in Riverdale, he looked hale and hearty enough.

Eventually, they got used to him and ended up voting him a Justice of the Peace, "*Judge* Moyers" if you don't mind, when he was probably about 40 years old or so. By then he'd taken a wife and they had four boys. One girl that died, too. Midwife couldn't make it out there in time and the babe was just too small, they said. His wife never recovered from heartache and he lost her, too. His boys were godawful young, so he packed them off to her parents back in Boston.

Now why I want you to know about him is this: There was something that happened that next springtime with him that this area ain't never gotten over. It's yours now, too, I guess, if you're staying among us.

There had been some talk about things happening out on the farms along Cricket Creek, not far from your place. Mostly women, all het up about livestock not acting right, some double-headed calves, dogs barking at nothing in the nighttime, cats hissing at shadows. That sort of thing. Well, a few began whispering, and some dared to speak louder still. Eventually, the rest of them worked it up into a lather and some started pointing fingers at old Molly Newell.

Now, Molly, she was widowed long-since and about 85 years old by then, and she stayed in her birth home. Maybe she'd teach a local girl to knit or make soap, maybe talk about how the towns was when she was young. But she lived alone, sometimes mumbled in the streets and had the gall to keep cats and an herb garden so when a few cattle had been found stumbling and leaking blood all over one morning it was enough for the rest of them waggle-tongues. Hmph.

The whole of Riverdale spent the day arguing on the porch of McClusky's market-- you know, down where the ice cream place is now, that used to be McClusky's, like a general store. By nightfall, even the men were worked up and scared and, prodded on by their wives and each other, about fifteen of 'em went down to Molly's, broke down the door when she wouldn't answer, and her huddled behind her bed at the sound of it. Dragged her off to the nearest boat and made for Moyers' Island to see about getting her hanged straightaway as a witch.

Judge Moyers knew as well as you that she wasn't a witch, but he saw murder and too much excitement in their eyes that night and didn't dare argue the point, not then. So he stalled. Said he ain't never presided over a witch trial and he wanted to do it properly, by the law. Needed to study up on it first in his books, probably pulled a few heavy ones down for show. Must have been enough to convince them. They left poor old Molly shaking in the corner of his study, hands still tied, and loaded themselves back into the boat.

When enough time had passed, Moyers quietly put Molly in a boat of his own, gave her what money he had at the house, bit of food, and pushed her off towards Pittsburgh hopin' she'd find peace.

Next morning, the townspeople figured out what he had done and were close to stringing him up instead. He must have used his lawyerly way with them and calmed them, but the people wouldn't talk to him anymore after that. No speaking to him in McClusky's. He paid his money quietly and left. No hat-tipping when passing him in the streets. And he didn't dare show himself in church again. That went without saying.

His law practice began to fail and the money ran out. He packed up his things, fetched his boys and moved down South. He was a humble man, quiet man. But I'll bet somewhere inside him, he thought he'd done right.

But let me back you up to that night Molly headed out on the water. Because what Moyers didn't see was that some men had been sitting up on the bank of the river watching his house, waiting for him to go to bed so's they could row back over and get the deed handled and be done with.

Those watchers moved out fast and quiet, and got Molly's boat when she'd gone too far for her cries to be heard. They strung her up brutally according to plan, on an island further downstream. She foamed and kicked, despite her age. They say it took her eight minutes to die. They cut her down and dug quickly.

The island they put her in was mostly mud. No one ever went there, not even fishermen stopping to take a dump. Can't imagine they marked the grave in any way. And none of them spoke about what they'd done. Not to their wives. Not to each other. Not to preacher nor priest.

But eventually, the crows told all.

One year the river flowed over, as it was fond of doing after a heavy winter thaw, and her purple bloat body came loose and floated down aways and off to one side where the crows wouldn't leave off picking at it. Some of the Riverdale boys had made their way down there for fishing and found her: rope stuck deep in the swell of her neck, black mourning dress she always wore. All of them knew it was Molly.

The boys came screaming back into town.

Stories were invented and accusations made. By then, the fever had passed enough for decent people to feel regret.

Years passed. People moved. Legends grew.

Parents would point to the rope hanging out over the island-- yeah, that's the one, the one you asked me about-- maybe use it to warn their children. Maybe, "Don't stay out too late or Ol' Molly's gonna getcha." Something like that.

I see you shifting in your chair, there. You think I was done? Did you think Ol' Molly's gettin' strung up and planted was the end of it? I wish it had been, son. I wish it had. When the internet took over, I began to see that it wasn't over, maybe never would be. I'm gonna fetch us both another beer before I tell you the rest, though.

One day it popped into my head, I'd just go and look up Riverdale or that old legend about the island and have a laugh. So I did that "Google" on it, and I saw something there I wish I hadn't.

Not a mention—not one—about what happened to Molly Newell.

Googling on "Riverdale" triggered a whole lot of old town photos and things. School classes, summer fairs. I printed a bunch of 'em out. Let me get 'em and you have yourself a look. I'll wait.

You seeing it now? Exactly. Same woman, every one. Never ages. This is some hundred years in photos I'm showing you.

I asked at the school. They've seen her around. Doesn't talk much. Maybe mumbles a bit. Harmless enough little old lady, said they just assumed she worked there. But here's 1890, 1930, 1960 and there she is. Watchin' us all. What's she doing at the school now and in this photo from 1890? I surely do not know. But that's why I said I think it isn't over. That and the cows.

Sheriff told me about your double-headed calf. Said it got pretty messy over there. That's half the reason I'm tellin' you this. Been happening some, as of late. You ain't the only one. It was really only a matter of time.

I don't know, Will. I don't know. Riverdale might not be the best place to be this year. I'm thinking you and your Amy might do best just to keep on passing through.

Author's note: This piece won 2nd prize at a writers' conference in Western Pa—Writing Success. I pass these islands in the Allegheny all the time. They just seemed to have something to say.

The story is based on reality: An older lady in 1804 was indeed dragged out to Twelve-Mile

Island in Harmarville, Pa, to answer for the crime of being a witch. The young magistrate hemmed and hawed and finally stalled the people by telling them he had to look up the pertinent laws in his books. When they left, he helped her escape. Likely, she lived. But I couldn't let it end so easily...

FESTIVAL

The end-of-winter festival blazes in the village below as I open my cabin door. From up here in the hills, there is much to see. I shiver and wrap my cloak about me, move silently behind trees to watch people prepare the day.

Bonfires as tall as men decorate the landscape. It is early, still, but the villagers huddle before them, bartering, exchanging what remains of their meager autumn harvests. No wafting scents of roasted meats reach me this festival. No laughter. No uproar of music and celebration.

Three men finger wooden whistles. There are only a few who pretend to dance steps.

At the center stands a thick pole. There is a man bound to this—by his ankles, by his middle, by his arms, by his neck.

He has been beaten, flayed beyond recognition to lie in pain a full day before they dragged him out to his death. Some say he didn't live that long. But ceremony would be followed.

Every villager lays a bundle of sticks at his feet. They spit in his blood-crusted face, "Riddance to you, John Haberman! And a curse upon your bones." Superstitious fools.

John Haberman has done nothing wrong. He has not harmed these people, has not stolen their livestock. His crime was to have had too large a harvest, in a village where having plenty is viewed with suspicion.

"Burn," came the verdict.

"He has seduced the gods of harvest. He has found favor with them," neighbors had accused. "He has been given our share of bounty."

"What I have is also yours," John Haberman protested, his words trembling though I knew his body did not. He believed the people would see reason.

But the people had stopped listening, and John Haberman was mistaken.

Village men began whispering on their boats, on their hunting excursions. Village women whispered as they gleaned their meager gardens, collected laundry from lines. Before Elder Smith had arrived from the city and pronounced sentence, the village had long decided the man's fate.

Elder Smith had John Haberman bound and held for festival night. His lands were burned. His children were sent back to his dead wife's village. They would be seen no more.

Elder Smith left the leaders of the village to carry out his instructions. The coward would bear no blood on his own hands.

I returned from two weeks foraging to find John Haberman's fate ordained.

I am grateful to be mostly ignored here in my hill home. I load my sled, tie it to my own waist. When there is hauling to do, I must do it myself. My cattle, too, were taken to fill bellies in the village. But I am fast, and I am strong.

I bless the snow. Without it, this journey would be impossible. On snow, I can pull. In mud, I stand no chance.

Wind is fluting through the trees, every twig plays a different angry note. It slices through my cloak and kirtle. It knots the hair I forgot to tie back, in my haste. New snow slaps my cheeks like an angry mother.

One mile, I can no longer smell the festival woodfires.

Two miles, there are no more footprints along the mountain paths.

Three miles, I am trudging slower. I cannot breathe this ice-air much longer.

Four miles. If the snow holds, this may be far enough.

I uncord my load and choose my spot as winter thunder echoes among the hills. I brace myself against an oak and use my legs to push it off the sled, down the hill.

My burden rolls five times before coming to a stop against two trees. It is the best I can do. I pack snow around it. I need to hurry back before his fires are lit.

I reach my cabin as a kind of frenzy takes hold of the village. Every man, woman, and child is throwing hate at the pole, at this man, this offering.

I grab my prepared torch, race down the path, praying they will not start without me.

There is plenty of time. I light my torch and stand among them, seething, waiting the signal. When it is given, I make sure my torch is the first on the pile. I stand among them an hour, making certain consumption will occur.

"It is good you have decided to join us, Greta," old Jasper Twining is staring at me. "Many of us wonder about you, up there alone in your cabin."

I break gaze from his leering eyes. My work is done, for now. It is time to return home.

I take my rest in the cabin for one more night.

Before dawn I bind my last few items to the sled. It is good I do not have much. I pat my cabin door on my way out. I have seen much from this cabin, but few have seen me. I say a prayer to thank the evergreens for their sure cover.

My feet find the path I followed yesterday. As I pass the four mile mark, I look down to the clump of trees where I packed snow to hug and hold him when I could not.

I toss near him the blood-stained leather flail I had used to exact whatever revenge was possible. Small consolation.

The wind still blows, still cuts into me like a dagger. But I am warm, remembering the fire and the smell of the flesh of Elder Smith.

Author's note: This piece won an honorable mention at Writers Weekly's Winter 2015 contest.

WILLING

He took no notice of the old lady clutching her walking stick, carefully choosing her path toward him as he strolled through the Saturday morning Market. Instead, he savored the yearn in the villager's eyes as they looked upon him.

He caught his name as they whispered when he passed. The sound was brushed velvet to him. The sound caught in the streams of their hair and called back to him. They wanted him. He made them *want* him.

This was a great pleasure for him: that they should despair for want of him. The thought had warmed him through the long winter.

He walked among the pine-and-canvas

merchant stalls, careful to stop at each. The men inside the stalls stepped back, unaware they were doing so. Their wives and daughters stepped forward, unaware *they* were doing so.

He was deliberate in movement, stroking a bolt of cloth here, carefully handling a dish there. He found that placing the items directly back into the hands of the shop-owner's wife produced just the reaction he wanted, a trembled smile. He himself smiled often, drinking their quiet gasps.

Every few stalls, he crossed the market entirely, giving all the chance to side-glance him. He ate eels-in-sauce, venison stews, roasted turnips, buying only a morsel at a time. He ate slowly, that they might watch him.

All the women of town would be in church tomorrow. Most of the men as well. He drew them all. For hours they would sit on polished oak, torn by the pleasure of being near him but unable to have more of him than anyone else. The heat from their longings would rise to him.

He manufactured stories for them: tales, warnings of submission, compliance, and the burn awaiting those who would not obey. They were distracted by the way the sweat of his skin glistened in his oratory, by the glow of stained glass sun on the black satin of his hair, by the music of his voice.

He would take several of them soon and be

gone to the next town due. Off through the misted nights that defined these northern riverlands.

These lands would renew. Another harvest in sixty years, seventy perhaps. When those young now would be too old to remember. Soft and sweet, new flesh would be born. Be his to take.

It was difficult to control himself, not to get greedy, for they all seemed so *willing* . . .

Old Marta remembered that morning why he looked so familiar. His face lodged in her thoughts like when she was so little and Papa would hum while he sewed shut holes in his fishing nets. Couldn't shake those songs for days.

Couldn't shake the picture of his face since she first made her way into town once winter had passed. His crow-black hair, eyes black as the bottom of a well, skin even paler than you would expect of a preacher and scholar.

The new Reverend, he didn't want to hear it when she said again she was sure he was familiar to her. He tried to hold his smile while the young ladies filed out the church doors but he hissed through his teeth, "We have spoken about this for the last time, Mrs. McKay."

She might have let it drop except this morning in the market place, he ran a hand through his hair and behind his left ear she saw it. Thick scar maybe two inches, jagged at one end. Memory poured through her.

Oh, he had done a fair job of hiding it, but she knew who he was. And she knew where that scar came from: she had given it to him. She turned and made for home with that realization, her eighty-year-old legs plodding straight and true despite the spring-thaw mud.

"My, but I was so young," she muttered to herself. "Still, I was quicker than a cat out of bathwater. But I *had* to be fast. That was my sister, my Grace, he made off with."

It had been Grace not long before, anyway.

She had stopped him back then, but he had returned. And he would surely return again. And again. He was harvesting their village as sure as a farmer planted and reaped his crops.

Arriving at her home, she dug under baskets, hoping her late husband hadn't removed what she'd once hidden there. He hadn't.

"Didn't sink it in deep enough the first time. Foolish old woman, do you think he'll hold still and let you try again?" she chided herself, closing her cottage door and steeling herself for the walk back to town.

She didn't worry he'd be gone from Market when she returned. She had seen how he took his time there. She knew now he'd been choosing. "Lingers for hours, he does, patting hands and smiling. Showing teeth," she thought.

"Them *teeth,*" she shuddered.

She held tightly to her walking stick as she navigated the small hill back into town. There stood the Reverend, surrounded by admirers. She made herself ready.

She approached, gently stroked his sleeve. "I need to speak with you." He grimace told her he was not pleased.

She leaned close and from beneath her apron pulled the same six-inch fishhook she had used some seventy years ago to beat him off Grace as his teeth had ripped and shredded her flesh. It was all she had. A fisherman's daughter uses what she can.

He sneered and spat, recognizing her trophy. Recognizing *her.* "Old woman, you will not last the day," he whispered his threat.

"No. I didn't intend to," she answered, sadly, drawing the hook up her *own* arm, releasing the crimson she knew would trigger his frenzy, expose him for what he was. He was on her immediately: sucking, devouring, revealing.

Author's note: This piece hasn't won anything, but my brother Vernon was fond of it, so I offer it here for him. I liked it, too. And no, I didn't imagine the guy to be a vampire. But everyone else did. So be it.

MOVING ON

Fred and Jean York pulled their RV into the picnic grove lined in lilacs, pines and firs. They had been working their way up the coast since leaving their San Francisco home two weeks before.

The trip had been Fred's suggestion. The Thursday they left home marked ten years since their daughter, son-in-law and five-year-old granddaughter Ingrid had been taken from them in a car accident the locals still talked about.

According to the skid marks left behind, Scott had been forced too close to the cliff's edge. The car spun, and there had been no guard rail.

The fire hadn't left much to bury.

Fred gathered their paper wrappers, crumpled them into a ball. He chucked them into the dying-down fire, which gave a "pop" to let them know it was still trying. That sound was echoed by a similar crack from within the near woods. He and Jean snapped heads toward the sound's direction.

A dark shape moved almost imperceptibly among trees. Raccoon? Large dog? Bear, even? Not unheard of here in Oregon. But not common, either.

Fred grabbed a piece of pie-crust from the full pan between them, threw it near the shape. No response. His hand found a small stone near his foot while his eyes fought to focus the shape. He tossed the stone, again no response. There was silence for a moment before Fred decided they'd been here long enough. Let whatever it was come scavenge.

He spoke as casually as he could. "Jean, dear, how 'bout you go see if we have more of that good coffee in the pot?"

Jean rose slowly, unwillingly, but Fred soothed her with a slight smile, never glancing away from the dark mass. "I'll be right there, darlin'," he nodded.

She crossed behind him while he felt around by his feet for the fire bucket. He doused the fire, then backed slowly. The thing shifted. It wanted what Fred and Jean were leaving behind.

Fred's hand found the side of the RV. "Here, love," Jean used her voice to lead him. He felt her slip her hand under his arm, guide him up the steps backwards into the RV. Jean slammed the door. Safe. She looked at him, shaking. Fred kept his shaking inside.

"It's not moving." Jean gestured out the side window.

"Nope. Well, let's move on. Let it have your pie, then." He nudged Jean. "Pro'bly follow us all the way to Seattle once it gets a taste of that."

Jean dared a weak laugh. They made their way to their seats, buckled and Fred started the motor. They were back to the comfort of the highway again in seconds.

Several towns later, Fred became braver and began joking about what they might have seen. "Could have been a wolf. But I'm betting on a Sasquatch. They're all over here. You can pick 'em up by the dozen, some of these smaller towns."

Jean gave the laugh he was looking for. She seemed to have calmed down. Fred turned on the radio. Frank Sinatra began singing about

"Strangers in the Night." Jean rolled her eyes and turned the station.

It was good, what the people had left. It was *good*.

She didn't remember it was called "pie." She wouldn't have cared, anyway. What mattered was getting it all into her stomach before competition crawled out from the woods.

Raccoons frequented this area as often as she did. She knew what to do if they posed a problem. She wouldn't have lived this long if she hadn't been able to follow her instincts, protect her food. A sharpened stick lay next to her. She was fast and had found many meals by spearing what approached her as she ate.

She wiped her hands on the stolen giraffe t-shirt she wore. She didn't remember it was called "giraffe." She didn't remember it was called a t-shirt. She didn't remember that she herself had once been called Ingrid.

The fair-haired teenager moved silently back through her woods. She balanced over the log bridge, crossing this same deep gully she had long ago crawled into after that terrible, terrible fire.

Author's note: This came from a writing prompt at a class I attend: Writers at Work. We were given a few elements to juggle: giraffe, San Francisco, the "pop" of a fire, Fred, Jean...

BARKING TOWN

If I can budge up the tiniest bit, I'll be able to see them again. Ah, better.

Now, I think that's the MacEwan boy jumping. I remember his mother. Couldn't punctuate to save her life, but a whiz with her math.

Can't imagine she'd be pleased to see her own boy jumping off those useless old bridge supports. Same ones where her own brother drowned, the lot of them whooping and hollering same as these boys. Smacked his head on the cement when he flipped, as I recall. But it wasn't what killed him. No.

Mark, that's this one's name. Mark MacEwan. Hmm. He must be about done with school now. Maybe this past year.

I could ask Mrs. Sherman if I could wake her up. She remembers these things. But it wouldn't be fair. She does so much for me, useless old lady that I am. Look at the sweet peace on her face, bless her. She does surely deserve a bit of a nap, if anyone does. Must be close to supper time, though, if I'm reading that lowered sun right. My, but I am hungry.

Someone ought to put a stop to it, all this river-swimming. I can't anymore, but *someone* ought to. Though I suppose kids these days need something to do around here, with the town as good as shut down. Keeps them out of trouble. My Thom always said I worried too much. I suppose he was right. Old Barking Town. Hmph. Never was much of a town. Not even when the mines were open. A few houses here and there, and those all but empty.

Mrs. Sherman told me that the population of Barking was once as high as 502. It's on the sign when she drives in. But that must have been in its heyday. I don't think Barking can have seen so many people in years.

Let's see. We lost the Morrissons year before last. Off to grab Florida sunshine, they were. It was the Kelsoes the year before. Or was that three years ago? Oh, dear. Muddle-headed me. The

Kelsoes are still here, I think. It's the Kesslers that left.

I can't get those boys out of my mind. Now, let me think. What year was it, when the four boys drowned? '81 or '82, I should think. Reagan was in the White House, then. Early days, still, for him. My, that was a sad summer around here.

Do you remember the terrible summer, Mrs. Sherman? Mrs. Sherman?

There I am again. I do forget myself. I'm so sorry. You sleep, dear.

Bit cold for these boys to be swimming in the Allegheny, I should think. September, is it already? October? I think it might just be October. Some of the leaves are starting to change. Must be an Indian Summer. Maybe Mrs. Sherman will prop a window for me when she's up.

It's a pity we never signed on for that Meals On Wheels. I do so hate the idea of disturbing poor Mrs. Sherman for supper. I didn't plan to get old. Funny to watch it happening.

Dear Mrs. Sherman's not much better off. I'm the only family she has left now, too. Just us two in the world. Bless her heart, she brings herself every day to sit here by me. The only one who does, now.

I don't think she even went home last night. In truth, I think it's as good for her as it is for me. Her own young ones left for the city, oh, years ago. Years ago. All these memories just start swirling again like the leaves there on the hillside. Windy it must be out there.

Well, my mind might not be much, but my eyes are as sharp as ever. And those boys are still jumping. Now, why would they do that? Why won't that MacEwan boy stay away from those cement pillars?

You would think his mother would have told him... but maybe she didn't. I never did hear them talk about the thing behind the pillars. The thing that bobbed and floated. The thing that watched. Now why was that?

I held my tongue. Figured the sheriff held information back sometimes. I know they do that in their investigations and I thought maybe I'd just keep it quiet for him, too. One of my best students, and there he was protecting us all. He was a good boy. College. Married. Two little girls of his own.

Oh, it's slipping away. I'm losing it again. I've got to try to hold onto it this time. The boys. It was something to do with those boys down there. Mark MacEwan. He's one of them. It was his uncle got taken under after he jumped. That was it.

Mrs. Sherman? Do you remember when that MacEwan boy's uncle drowned? Mrs. Sherman?

He drowned. No, he *didn't* drown. He didn't drown, but everyone thought he did. He hit his head when he jumped. I saw it from here. But it wasn't what killed him. It was the thing hid behind those pillars.

It was floating, like driftwood, maybe it even hung to a piece of driftwood. I can't recall. But it ducked under the water just as that boy hit the water, all bloodied. I wasn't sure what it was, though my eyes are good as ever. I never had cataracts like Mrs. Sherman or my Thom. No.

Now, that looks like the MacEwan boy down there. I wonder why someone doesn't stop those boys jumping off there. Don't they know the danger? Don't they know how those boys were taken all those years ago? My, but it was *hungry*. I never told anyone. It was the sheriff's right to hold back what he wanted.

Took them all: One, two, three, four, as they jumped. Oh, why did they keep jumping? That was it-- they were looking for him. Looking for the first boy. The other MacEwan boy. They saw him hit his head and then they were in the water, too, *looking* for him. Not a one of them ever came up again.

Sheriff found their clothes, shoes. I think the story in the papers said it was the undercurrent pulled them all under and they never found a body. Not a bone. Because it had been hungry.

Hungry. Did we have breakfast? I can't remember.

I don't think Mrs. Sherman is getting up again, and it's a shame. It's a shame. Because he is down there again.

I think he's been there all afternoon, hiding there behind those rocks, watching them. Watching those boys jump.

It's moving now. Oh, it's *moving*.

Oh, someone needs to warn those boys there's *something* in that water.

Author's note: There's a little community on the opposite side of the river from me: Barking. It was once a thriving little mining town, but these days it's abandoned. Mostly. My son and I were on our side of the river one day and happened to see a pack of boys whooping and hollering and jumping off pylons into the river. It was a gorgeous cold day, not one for swimming. This piece was originally printed at Black Poppy Review, in September of 2015.

BROTHERS THREE

This stone bench is cold and Brother-beside-me and I, we shift uncomfortably. We cannot see Brother-behind-us, but he speaks and we do as he says.

"Nearer the door," he commands, and we shuffle our feet until we have moved us closer to their door.

From inside, I hear a whisper ask what is to be done with us three, now the Abbess has been Gathered Unto God so tragically.

"Sister Claire is asking the others about us," I tell them, as my ears are now closest. "And there is fear in her voice."

"We put them OUT," Sister Mary Agnes spits, and though we cannot see her, we know that her face is red, her eyes angry and tight. The flab of her neck shakes when she speaks. "They should have been dropped in the towns ages ago."

Because she thinks we cannot hear her, she adds, "Or in the well."

Some Sisters snicker at this.

Sister Mary Agnes told us many times she had counseled the Abbess to leave us in the snows that surrounded this mountain monastery at our birth nine years ago.

"Oh, but perhaps they were meant to teach us. How like the Holy Trinity they are -- three boys in one body," timid Sister Margaret dares. "The third just showing forth behind the other two, so spirit-like."

"And yet," snaps Sister Mary Agnes, "Not a one of us can bear the sight of them, yourself included, Sister Margaret. It is a pity the Abbess wasted so much of her strength caring for them."

Sister Mary Agnes will meet her end easily out the tallest tower in a fortnight, we decide. She is even older and lighter than the Abbess was.

We smile holy smiles as the Sisters file from the room.

Author's note: Love a good tight Flash Fiction. You saw in Small Onya what I did to those poor conjoined twins? So, of course, I lay awake at night wondering if there have ever been conjoined triplets. This was published at Black Poppy Review, March 2015.

TRAVELER

It was her sister Maisie who noticed him first.

She double patted Annie's shoulder just after the bells rang over the door of Father's General Store. It was their silent signal for, "Look now but don't say anything." And no wonder her older sister tapped her, Annie smiled.

A city man, to be sure, by his suit. Well-off city man, or she was no judge of a cut of cloth. Probably traveling out West, as they all seemed to be these days. There was money out there, and certainly none to be had here in an old trading post in Missouri.

Annie glanced in the glasspane behind the

counter, smoothed a few curls, and turned back to watch him. She tried not to linger her gaze, careful not to let the few other townspeople in the shop notice her watching him.

She needn't have worried. Mrs. Hadley, the undertaker's wife, held up two choices of cloth to her distracted husband. Jimmy Bailey was almost drooling over the jars of candy that lined the shelves. No one bothered to look at her.

The man was thin and lanky, his movements stiff, a shuffling walk; but that was to be expected when traveling distances by coach. His hair must have been a gentle brown, but was slicked and oiled in the city-style of the day. His hands lingered over canned foods, bottled goods, as though he meant to pick them up, but he did not.

Maisie pulled their shared school-slate and chalk closer, wrote, and passed to Annie: "ASK IF HE'S PASSING THROUGH OR STAYING."

Annie reddened and shook her head. She was never so bold as Maisie. She giggled and tittered at the thought of such presumption.

"A good evening to you, sir. Is there something special we can help you find?" Maisie hailed him as Annie quietly pressed her own shoe onto her sister's foot.

Maisie pushed her hard away, sending Annie into the suspended scales. Annie righted herself, bit her tongue to avoid speaking the words she'd have liked to have said to Maisie, and watched the man's reaction from the corners of her eyes. There was none.

She moved toward the board, erased it with the dusty slate-rag and wrote, "FOREIGN? OLD COUNTRY?"

Maisie shrugged and tossed her head. Annie choked back a laugh. She knew Maisie's spurned look. There weren't many young men in town who would ignore Maisie Anderson's attention. She sulked when she found one who would.

Annie turned her attention back to the inventory books, pausing occasionally to watch the man. His skin was pale as clotted cream, almost a grey. He was probably a scholar. Or a clerk. Perhaps a banker. Yes, a banker. That would explain the fine fabrics he wore.

At last, the silent man approached, set a small pair of thread snippers on the counter and placed two coins into Annie's hands, pennies. "Thank you," she said, still too shy to look in his face until just as she handed him his purchase. She looked up at him and stopped breathing.

The man's eyes held no color. They were cloud-white. He held Annie's gaze a few moments, then stretched the tightest grin full across his face. A brown thread hung from the corner of his lips.

Her insides iced over.

He took the snippers, opened them slightly, and ran their twin blades between his lips, brown threads dropping to the counter before her. He turned and left the store as wordlessly as he'd arrived.

Maisie spoke over her shoulder, still petulant. "Cat got his tongue, I s'pose. Too good for town girls." She sniffed and went back to straightening cans.

In the back corner of the shop, Mr. Hadley cleared his throat. Annie jumped, realizing he had been studying the scene. "May I see those coins, Miss Annie?" he asked her.

She pulled them off the shelf of the till and held them out to him. He pulled them closer, examined them.

"That's what I thought," he told her. "Same ones I placed on his eyes late last night." He handed back the coins and moved to the front window, looking up the road where the traveler had walked. "Mebby you girls want to lock up shop and head home for the night."

Author's note: I worked in retail for some time. Across the street was a cancer-specializing medical center. Many people shopping at our store had a grey tinge to their appearance as they fought the worst of it. A young man came in one day, though, who was the purest grey. He barely spoke, if at all, when checking out. There was something unearthly about him, which is why he ended up in here. Printed at Black Poppy Review, October 2015.

SHOELACE

Having finished most of my shopping, I turned left by the bluejeans, walking slower to the back of the store toward the shoes. Using the overhead mirrors, I watched where I had been. Sure enough, *she* made the turn, too.

Her long, crinkly grey hair pinned up in a French roll, head down, she pretended to examine a pair of Levi's while every now and then lifting her head, watching me. This woman seemed to be turning up in every aisle I was in, no matter how far I had come across-store. She was very tiny, very wrinkled, very pale. Dressed in a very Victorian shade of grey-violet velvet, she looked every bit an old English widow.

I had no idea who she was, and had only noticed her about five minutes before when I first bumped into her back in the groceries, standing back up from tying my blasted shoelaces. The shoelaces were the primary reason for my shopping trip. They'd rarely come untied in the year since I'd bought them, but lately they were doing it several times a day. I'd considered chucking them out entirely, treating myself to a new pair, but the shoes themselves had just reached the perfect stage of broken-in. Anyway, it wasn't the fault of the shoes so much as the worn-down laces.

The old woman was closing the distance to me. I wondered whether I should call her bluff and speak to her, maybe scare her off a bit, let her know I know she's following me.

Idea: I stopped, glanced around for whoever had brought her. Her hobble made it clear she could not have made the trip here alone. This little suburban mall was ten miles from anything. Surely a family member? A caregiver? But I saw none. All these thoughts passed quickly through my mind, and I had decided to finish and head out until...Oh, good grief! Shoelace AGAIN. This was getting ridiculous. Bend down, tie, double tie, stand up.

She was standing directly in front of me.

She smelled of garlic and lavender, both of which seemed to rise directly from the deep folds of her ancient ridged skin. Her look was apologetic, forehead wrinkled in that distinctive way that hints at pleading. Her eyes were the exact shade of Pennsylvania coal. They were wet, but not crying-wet.

She reached for my hand and I let her take it. She held it between her too-cool, creviced hands. "You can't see it, can you?"

Her voice was stronger, smoother than it should have been for all her years. A smoker's gravel-gargled voice would have sounded right. I wasn't sure whether to play along and humor her by saying "yes," or own up to the truth—I had no idea what she was talking about.

"Uh...I don't think so. What do you mean?"

"It's there," she gestured at my foot. "On your shoe. Any pain in that foot yet?"

I shook my head no, my heart pounding its discomfort in my ears.

"I saw it hanging off the side of that shoe as soon as you walked in," her face beamed. Her delight was obvious. "Dare say it's been there a while, now. May I?"

"What? You want my shoe?"

But she had already begun to bend down, catching at a nearby counter for balance. I took her arm to help, and she looked a smile up at me. "Yes, dear. Thank you. That's right."

She was squatting now, a bit breathless from her descent. People were beginning to turn curious glances our way. I made my best helpless shrug at them, mouthing, "I don't know?" by way of apology.

On the floor, she opened her purse and pulled out pliers? Wire cutters? She set to work on the side of my shoe.

Correction: she never actually touched my shoe. She was clipping away at the air near my shoe and humming something that called to my mind old hymns. I was just beginning to get my head around this when the fullest pain I had ever known shot through me: foot to leg to hip to trunk to neck to head.

"Jesus! She's cutting me!" I thought. I gasped in air, preparing to use it to scream when the pain stopped. Not only stopped—had *never been*. Nor was there any residual pain—nothing to indicate I had just been chunked open and bled by a velvet-and-grey granny on the floor. My shoe was whole, as was the foot inside.

She looked up at me, smiling sweetly, face shining all pride like a schoolchild's first A.

"And here it is," she showed me a nothing in a jar that might have been used for canning jellies. She held the jar to me and I took it, gave it a little shake. Nothing.

"Ahhh..." I said, not knowing what was expected of me, but hoping it was enough to make her go. This woman was clearly insane. What had she done down there? Poked me with a nail file? Mini taser?

She made a move to rise and instinctively I grabbed at her elbow, helping her to her feet.

She held out her hands, and I placed the jar in them again. She giggled a little, eyes huge as she enjoyed her prize. She cradled the jar in the crook of her arm, close to her body, and used her other hand to root through her handbag. She pulled forth a $100 bill as wrinkled as she, and nudged it toward my hand.

"I know it should be more, dear, but it's all I have."

I shook my head and pulled back. "I don't want your money—why are you giving me this?" In panic, I looked around in case a family member materialized and thought I was trying to dupe the woman of her savings.

"Shhh, now, dear. This is between us. You're not to tell a soul. And honestly, Ellie, who would believe you, anyway?" With that last, just for the briefest of moments, the kindly-widow look disappeared from her face in favor of a flash of sneer and it occurred to me that in reality she was nowhere near as helpless as she appeared.

I snatched the money and turned, abandoning my shopping cart, keeping my head down and walking as quickly as I could to the exit.

I turned back—how could I not? It was just in time to see her opening the jar, tipping it into her mouth, pounding the bottom to make sure she got it all.

I left then and haven't been back since. I have no interest in running into her again. Anyway, I haven't needed to go back. Those laces never came untied again.

Author's Note: This is an early piece, published in a slightly different form on Fireside Fiction's website. I think it was the first piece for which I was paid. Impossible to overstate what that did for my confidence. Thanks, Fireside! Original piece was edited by Brian J. White at Fireside.

When I was young, I went to a Christian fundamentalist school. One day, a "healer" visited. There was a large prayer service and I was told to go forward and get prayer for my ear infections.

I stood elbow-to-elbow with people in the church who had real concerns: cancer, diabetes. I felt a little silly, to be honest. When the healer came to me, he said he could see a little demon hanging off the side of my left earring.

Well! That was some pretty exciting stuff, frankly! I wanted to hear more about it but he prayed quickly and moved to the next-in-line. Here's the kicker: I never had another ear infection.

Fast forward thirty years: I had a shoelace that seriously would NOT stay tied. I wondered what was causing it, and the image of a little demon hanging onto my shoestrings rose up...

DRUM

There is one bright dancer among them. Her hands trace the music onto air. The "U" of her hips sways, telling bedroom stories. Melodies float her toward the youngest doumbek player, barely bearded.

She bends to him, smiling, flirting even, to the ululating tongues of all her watching sisters but as the Hafla pauses to draw a collective breath, I see the truth: her focus is not the drummer. She shines for the pulled-skin drum.

An elderly man leans near me. "It is all that remains of her husband."

"He played?" I am confused.

He shrugs. "He had enemies."

Author's note: I went to a Middle Eastern Hafla once and was enchanted by the colorful scarves, mystic music, and exotic foods. This piece was first printed at entropy2: 100 word short stories.

PAID

Ma wouldn't speak to me mostly that last long day. She just crumbled dried parsley, grated all manner of roots into that black-iron pot on the stove for our final meal together. Wouldn't look at me none, neither.

But I looked at her. I hid behind Papa's hanging old barn coat, the only thing that still held his smell, and I saw her hushing up her tears in her apron, and her lookin' around first to see if I was near. Finally sent me to sneak on Reverend Brown, see if folks were moving up our way yet.

No one much was gathered at Reverend Brown's. I walked my secret woods-path home. The sun was goin' down fast tonight. It didn't want to be here when He came.

The sun wasn't the only thing hurryin'. A flow of spiders, centipedes, half-crawlers, every color and size of snake, worms. All pushed past me. Couldn't get out of Summerdale fast enough to please 'em. I heard no birds. Saw none of the squirrels, deer or mice that ran so thick in these woods. They had long-left.

I saw Ma standing, waiting at the cabin window. Bet she already knew. But I ran in anyway.

"Ma! Come quickly!" I wanted her to see what things were making their way across the front lawn.

"I know. I know what's comin'. I know Who is comin'. You get over here now. Come look at me."

I stood before her.

She tipped up my chin, held my face. Her thumb carefully covered the mark He put on my cheek a year and a day ago. She looked me in the eyes, directly. Parts of her face were musclin' and twitchin' funny. Her voice was tight.

"I want you to know that whatever happens tonight, I am your Mama. I did not wish this on you. This was them." I nodded, then she held me so hard I felt all her bones press through.

We ate soup in silence.

Not long after, we heard voices outside. They were gathering. Reverend Brown put himself outside our front window.

I knew He would be among them. And He was. I went cold as creekstones to see him. Him with the slick black hair. Him with the too-wide smile. Him with the eyes that could swallow.

Reverend Brown spoke first, in a shout. Like he was in charge of something. "You surely do know *why* we're here. You bring her on out, now. We got to pay what's due." His last line held the hint of a shake. Of course it did. He was standing next to Him.

Ma shouted right back, "You give me a minute, Edward Brown. He'll have her soon enough. You give me my one more minute."

She wouldn't look me full-on. "You saw what He did to your Papa and Old Jonathan."

I nodded.

"You do as He says. I don't think He's looking to hurt you, if you do as you're told."

I nodded again, but not because I believed her.

"He picked you. Out of all of them. He picked you. Now, that's gotta count for somethin'."

I didn't say that He surely picked me for what Papa tried to do to Him after He cut Old Jonathan top-to-bottom. Anyway, it wasn't me she was trying to convince.

"Let's get out there, then." We stepped out into the moonlight.

Reverend Brown held out his hand for me to take. Suppose he intended to look like he was presenting me to Him on behalf of the town. I ignored that hand, walked to where He waited, pushing down the sick I felt.

He turned and walked into the forest. I followed, distracted by the silence. It wasn't until I tripped on a fir-tree root that I saw and smelled the hole. I knew my woods. This hole had not been here before. I would surely have noticed the stink that rose from it, all dead-deer gasses and bile.

His ice-hands grabbed me and pulled. We were both falling. Some mercy caught my hand, gave me a root to hold and I kicked, hard. This caught Him in the face. Knocked Him deeper into his own hole. I worked my way back up.

I heard Him laugh behind me.

I ran, gasping. Ma's cabin was ahead. The people were gone. I threw myself against our door, rattled the handle. Locked. I slapped the door, pounded the heel of my hand into it.

Ma answered. My Ma, in ruffles. My Ma, plump and smiling. "Hello?"

A bald man walked up behind her. He wore the finest suit with a gold watch and chain. "Darling? Who's there?"

"I was just waiting for her to tell me that. What can I do for you, dear? It's awfully late."

I couldn't breathe, let alone speak. I started to press into the house.

"Pardon us, Ma'am," He had come up behind me. I froze. "My missus seems to have the wrong house." He smiled his too-wide smile.

Ma nodded a "Goodnight," and gently pushed me out the door.

I heard the lock slide into place.

Author's note: I'm a mom. Nothing scares me more than a betrayal of the bond between parent and child. This piece won 3rd prize in Writers Weekly's Autumn 2013 24-hour contest. My first monetary prize!

A FISHERMAN'S TALE

The summer's fishing had not been kind to Brandr. Nor the spring prior to that. Finna herself was hungrier than ever, her swollen belly pushing the table every time she sat. Another child was well on the way. Brandr hoped for a seventh boy and made what sparse offerings he could afford to the gods in that hope. But as of late, the gods seemed to have turned their backs on him.

Brandr picked his way up the path between cliffs that lined the waters careful not to catch his shoe on the thick sea-sprayed mosses that favored these rocks. He trudged the hill homeward, empty. Nothing to take to market. The other men of the village steered their boats to the far part of the harbor, closer to market. It was easier this way, their nets straining to contain their haul. Only a short year before, Brandr would have been among them, joking and unloading while the youngest boys of the village raced to be the first to help bring the catch ashore.

But these days, he found he was no longer welcome among the men. His bad luck might be catching. They became quiet and elbowed one another when he passed. All laughter and joking stopped when he walked near. Silence, but for winds and water. Instead, village hands busied themselves, stretching forth nets to be repaired before putting out again to sea before the next dawn. The eyes of those too old to fish looked down at their table-work as they cut open the catch, gutting and cleaning to dry some of the day's bounty to put-by for winter.

Sparse wisps of smoke drifted from the chimney of Brandr's lone cottage in its place upon the cliffs, unlike those too-close cottages in the village, clustered and almost huddled together for warmth from the winter winds that would begin very soon. The chimney smells reached him now, bringing forth the scent of seaweed soup for yet one more night. Their own supply of dried fish had run out in the early part of spring.

He came in as quietly as he could, but the boys saw him and ran to his side, the older ones helping off his coat, the younger ones pleading the dreaded question: "How many fish today, Fadir?"

To this he gave no answer but continued to

pull off his boots, rubbing his feet. The older boys, glaring, punched their brothers who dared ask.

Finna squatted at the fire stirring, scooping and handing bowls. She smiled at Brandr all the way to her eyes and handed him the largest steaming bowl. He noted every day there was more seaweed and less from their tiny garden. But the coming winter sea could not continue to be generous.

Brandr's face greyed over at this thought.

He turned away from Finna that night in bed, ashamed to face her. Turned his face instead toward the wall that sided the sea. Finna reached over and stroked his hair, kissed the back of his neck. "I will go tomorrow and see wise Ingfrid. She will tell us how to restore your luck."

Brandr was quiet. He did not wish to be in debt to a witch. His whisper held great reluctance. "You know we cannot pay her."

Finna shrugged, untroubled. "She will pay herself—we will give her half the fish she helps you to bring in!"

The following evening as he walked through his door, Finna caught his eye with a small nod and tight, nervous smile. There was much to do. She sent the boys to collect wood for the night's fire while she whispered, hoarse, to him over soup, drawing with her finger on the table.

Next morning, Brandr awoke much earlier than usual, picked his way carefully to the beach, sliding down sometimes in his haste to begin his morning's work. He readied his boat and made as though to leave in it, but then paused and looked around. Surely it was time.

He walked the strand of the beach, picking up many small rocks and piling them near his boat. The pile grew as an hour passed, two hours. He had enough. He began placing them in the sand, almost in full circles around an empty center. Some of these curves he connected with others. Some he left alone, uncompleted.

When Brandr's work was finished, he stood back and had the thought that what he had created looked rather like the ripples of waves that came forth when a stone was tossed into the sea on a fair-weather day.

Following Ingfrid's careful instructions, he now entered his labyrinth slowly, giving the fey that were plaguing him time to follow. When he reached the center, he paused a moment, then jumped as far as he could, outside his many circles and ran for his waiting boat.

He pushed off, paddling as hard and fast as he could, the sea heavy on his oars. Hopeful. He knew the fey could not cross or leap the lines of the labyrinth as could he. It might take them hours to work their way out. Brandr paddled until he was so far from shore that even the cliffs of home could no longer be seen.

Brandr walked quickly up the hill to home late, late that night, laughing sometimes as he slipped the mosses. It had taken extra time to row toward market and unload, so full was his boat of fish of all kinds. He had stopped in the village to let some of the men buy him drinks. It had taken longer than he had thought. He rejoiced in the many coins in his pocket, the more that were coming.

He had just crested the hill when a figure emerged from their cottage. A few steps closer and he recognized Ingfrid carrying a small wrapped bundle. She turned in his direction, wrapped her shawl tighter around the bundle. She faced him, defiant, then spun toward her home beyond the village and stalked away.

Brandr stood, watched her for many minutes, then went inside where six boys were already sleeping. He climbed in to bed next to the now-empty, weeping Finna, stroked her hair, kissed the back of her neck.

Seated before her fire in her own cottage,

Ingfrid drew the child nearer to her. Few questions would be asked by people in the village. They remembered well what had happened to those who had dared to question Ingfrid before.

The child slept, sated for now by goat's milk. A seventh son. It had been an easy enough process, leading the fey to Brandr the previous spring.

She felt no pangs of conscience. It was the best possible outcome for all concerned—who better than she, she justified herself, to bring up a seventh son? She would know how best to further his abilities. He would never starve in her cottage. He would know and even play with his brothers. Secrets weren't easily kept in a small village. And as for Brandr and Finna, well it certainly wouldn't be long before they added an eighth, ninth, and tenth child to their home. Ingfrid thought she might even slip Finna some herbs to speed the process along.

The child stirred slightly. She picked him up, holding him in the firelight and began to sing...

Author's note: I love all things Nordic. I even do historical re-creation of the time period, so when the opportunity arose to contribute a piece to an anthology of Nordic tales, I jumped! This piece was originally printed in Folklore: The Northlore Series by Nordland Publishing, MJ Kobernus, ed. Much thanks to my dear friend Ambros Kyrielle for sharing his love of historical labyrinths with me!

End note

While my younger brother, David, got me writing, it was my older brother, Vernon, who kept the fires lit. He's been among my greatest champions, the one who knows how to format, print, sell. This is an end-dedication to him, too. With so much thanks.

Laura Lovic-Lindsay

Interested in More?

If you enjoyed this book, I have the beginning of a website started at http://talesthecrowstaughtme.com/. I will have a link to a larger piece I wrote, based on my small hometown.

Please join my mailing list to be notified of new books and poems as they become available.

Thank you so much for your patronage! I would rather write books than anything in the world, but life seems to have other dues to pay first. Please be patient with me for new material!

Cheers!

Laura Lovic-Lindsay

Made in the USA
Middletown, DE
17 May 2021